No other Fish Like Me

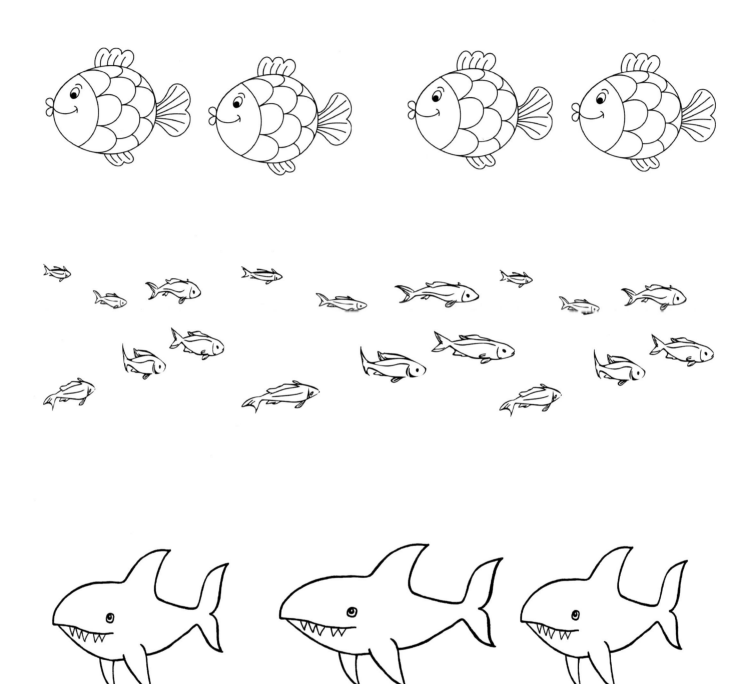

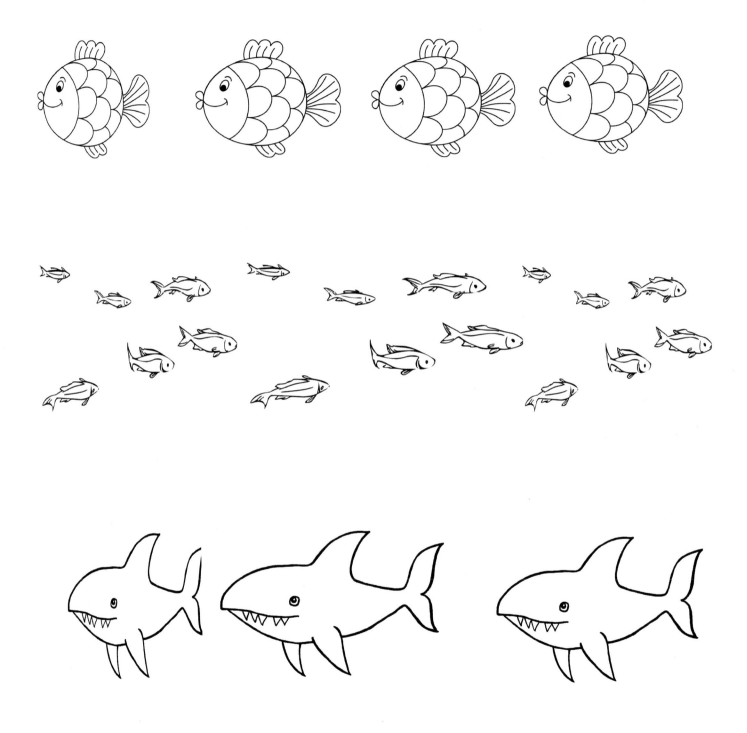

Book written in 2016 by author

Illustrations done in 2017

Published in January 2018

No other fish like me

By Tiffany Ward

Editor Lori Table

There once was a boy name Eli, who
loved to swim. Eli loved to swim so much
his mother brought him some fins.

Eli! His mother yelled, " with those fins you

are sure to turn into my little fish".

Eli loved the idea of being a fish so much he

said "mom I really want to visit the sea! I

want to see if those fish are just like me".

They both chuckle, "ha ha!"

"Oh there's no fish like you, but we can go to

the boat to see if that's true, "said his mom.

Eli was so excited! he hurried up and put

his fins on and ran around the house. After

a while he asked his mom if he could

practice holding his breath

underwater like a fish.

"sure, As long as I can count!" his mother

answered.

Eli quickly ran upstairs and got into the tub.

"1..." Eli could hear her say from under the

water. "2,3,4... keep holding your breath.

5,6,7,8,9,10!"

Eli jumped out the water with excitement.

"Yay" his mom screamed, "10 whole seconds!"

Eli quickly went to bed excited about

tomorrow's big adventure!

The next day Eli woke up bright and

early and yelled with excitement, " wake up

mom! we have to pack for the trip!"

Eli and his mom made Peanut Butter and Jelly

sandwiches just in case they got hungry. He

also packed his fins and goggles to see the

fish under water.

As Eli and his mom cruised through the sea, he thought to himself, "wow there's a lot of fish in the sea, but like mom said none of them are like me." "I see big fish, little fish, school fish, even clear fish that sting, but like mom said none of those fish are me".

Eli put his head in the water as a tropical

fish was going by. "Hey TROPIC!" Eli yelled!

"Yea," tropic answered.

"There are a lot of fish in the sea

but none like me!" Said Eli.

"How so" tropic wondered.

"Well I can sit in the sun, I can swing

from trees, and I hate grass!"

"That's so cool" said tropic.

Eli came up for a breather, and decided

he was hungry. He quickly pulled out his

peanut butter and jelly sandwich. Just

when he was about to take a bite, a big

seagull came flying along.

Hey seagull" Eli yelled!

"yea" said seagull

"there are a lot of fish in the sea" Eli replied

sure, sure " said seagull sneaking closer to Eli's

sandwich.

Before Eli could get another word out, the

seagull snatched Eli's sandwich and quickly flew

away yelling " and I am not one of them."

Eli slowly put his head back in the water. He was

sad about the Seagull taking his

sandwich. As he continued looking, he saw a school

of fish passing along.

"Hey school Fish!" Eli yelled very, very loudly.

"Yea," They all answered.

"There's a lot of fish in the sea but none like me!"

"How so?" Replied the school fish.

"Well I am the only child and I go to school all by myself".

"well that's nice, we have to go, Sharkey the shark is coming!" screamed The school fish.

Along came Sharkey moving rapidly behind the school of fish.

"Hey Sharkey!" Yelled Eli.

"What?" Sharkey replied, with a very angry voice.

Eli shouted "None of these fish are like me".

"Sure they are! I want to eat them and you too."

Well you can't eat me!" Eli replied.

Why not?" Screamed Sharkey.

Eli calmly told Sharkey, "I don't eat fish, I walk to school alone, I can jump, I can dance, and I climb trees, so you can't eat me!"

"Well what kind of fish are

you...!" asked Sharkey.

"Yea!" Yelled the school of fish.

"Yea," said tropic.

"Well I'm just me, and mom was

right, none of you fish are

anything like me!"

Mom turned to Eli and said, "well son it's time for

our trip to come to an end."

"It sure is mom, and I can't wait to do this

again!"

<u>Dedication</u>

This book is dedicated to my sons Eric, Kobe, and Eli I want you all to know that you're one of a kind and each of you are special in your own little ways.

I Love you!

To Chase
You Are Special
LOVE Tiffy

About the Author

My name is Tiffany Ward. I am a up and coming Author from North Philadelphia, with a big heart and a even bigger imagination. My stories are inspired by my sons, nieces, nephews and my passions for teaching self-love. I hope you enjoyed the story, and always remember love yourself. Thanks for reading!

Made in the USA
Lexington, KY
06 September 2018